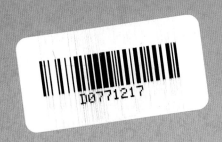

This book is dedicated to

my mother, who said I'm her flamingo,
my son, who arrived when I completed this book,
and my grandma in heaven, who gave me the happiest childhood.

Many thanks to Lee Wade, Rachael Cole,
and Isabel Atherton for all of your support
to make this book happen.

 Published in the United States by
Random House Studio, an imprint of Random House Children's Books,
a division of Penguin Random House LLC, New York.

Random House Studio with colophon is a registered trademark
of Penguin Random House LLC.

Visit us on the Web! rhcbooks.com
Educators and librarians, for a variety of teaching tools,
visit us at RHTeachersLibrarians.com

Library of Congress Cataloging-in-Publication Data is available upon request.
ISBN 978-0-593-12731-5 (trade) – ISBN 978-0-593-12732-2 (lib. bdg.)
ISBN 978-0-593-12733-9 (ebook)

The text of this book is set in 17-point KG Primary Penmanship 2.
The illustrations were rendered in Photoshop, watercolor, and colored pencil.
Book design by Rachael Cole

MANUFACTURED IN CHINA
10 9 8 7 6 5 4 3 2 1
First Edition

the FLAMINGO

by Guojing

RANDOM HOUSE STUDIO
NEW YORK

part one

A Trip to Visit Lao Lao All on My Own

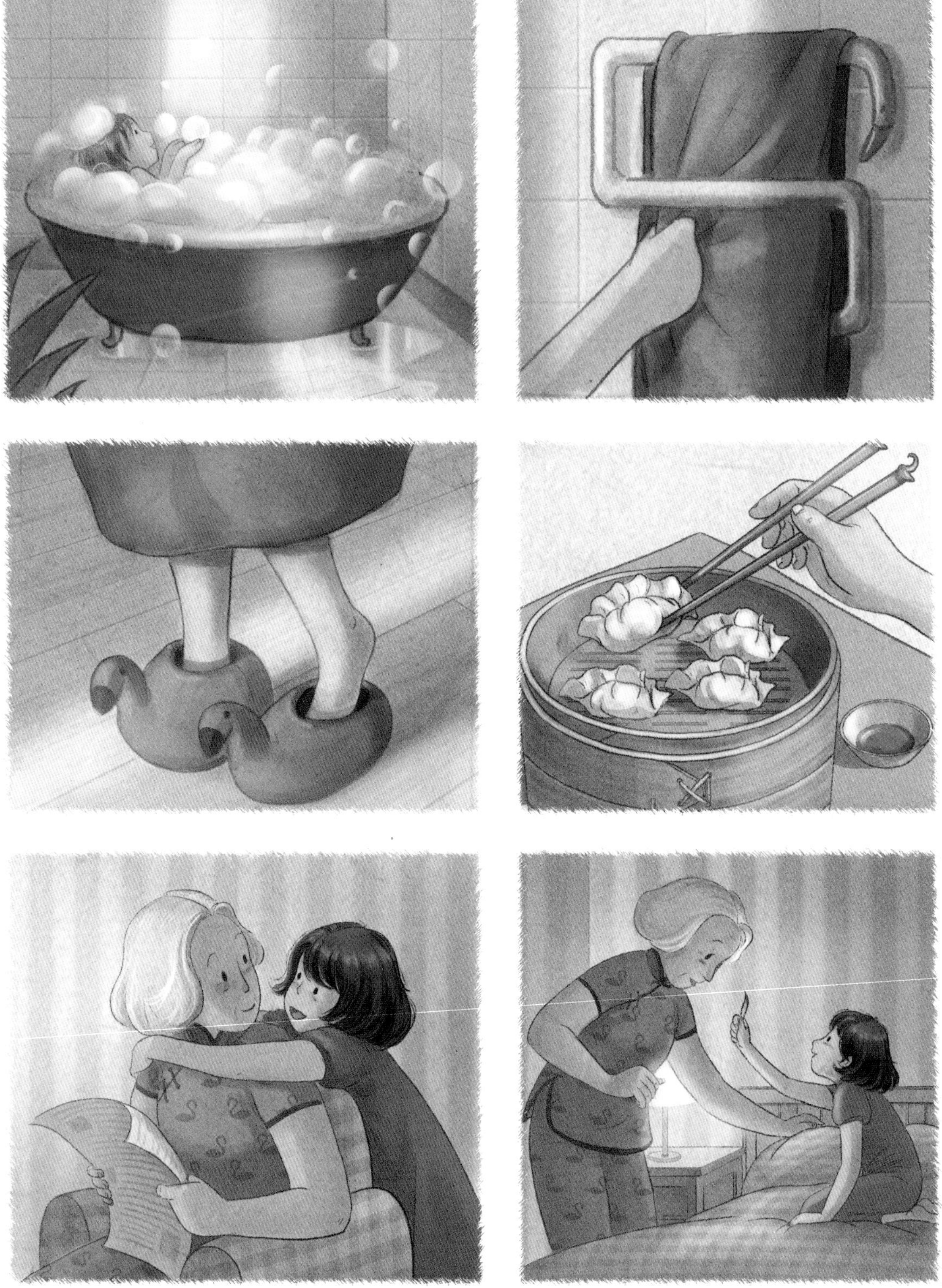

"Can you tell me about the feather?" I asked Lao Lao.

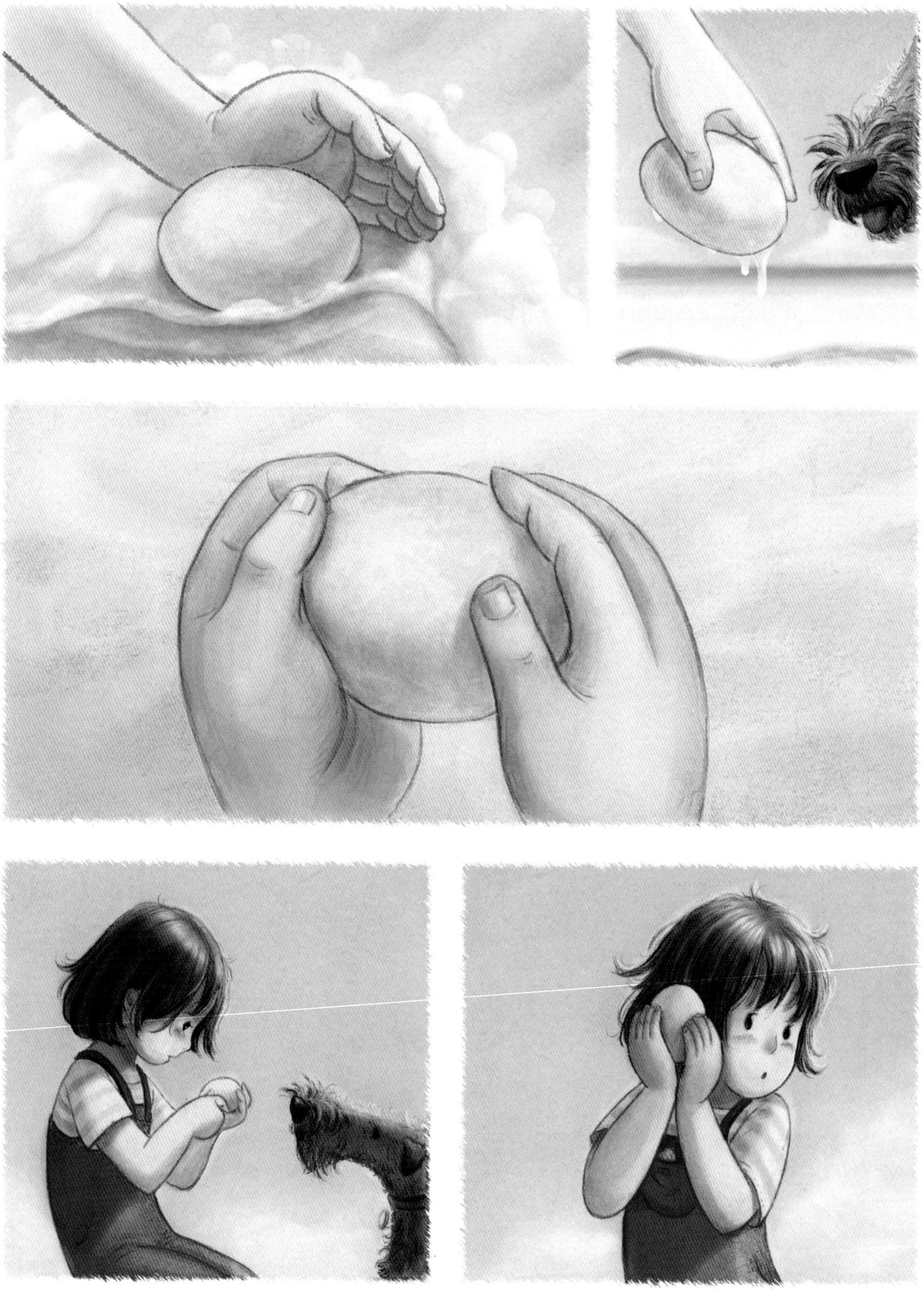

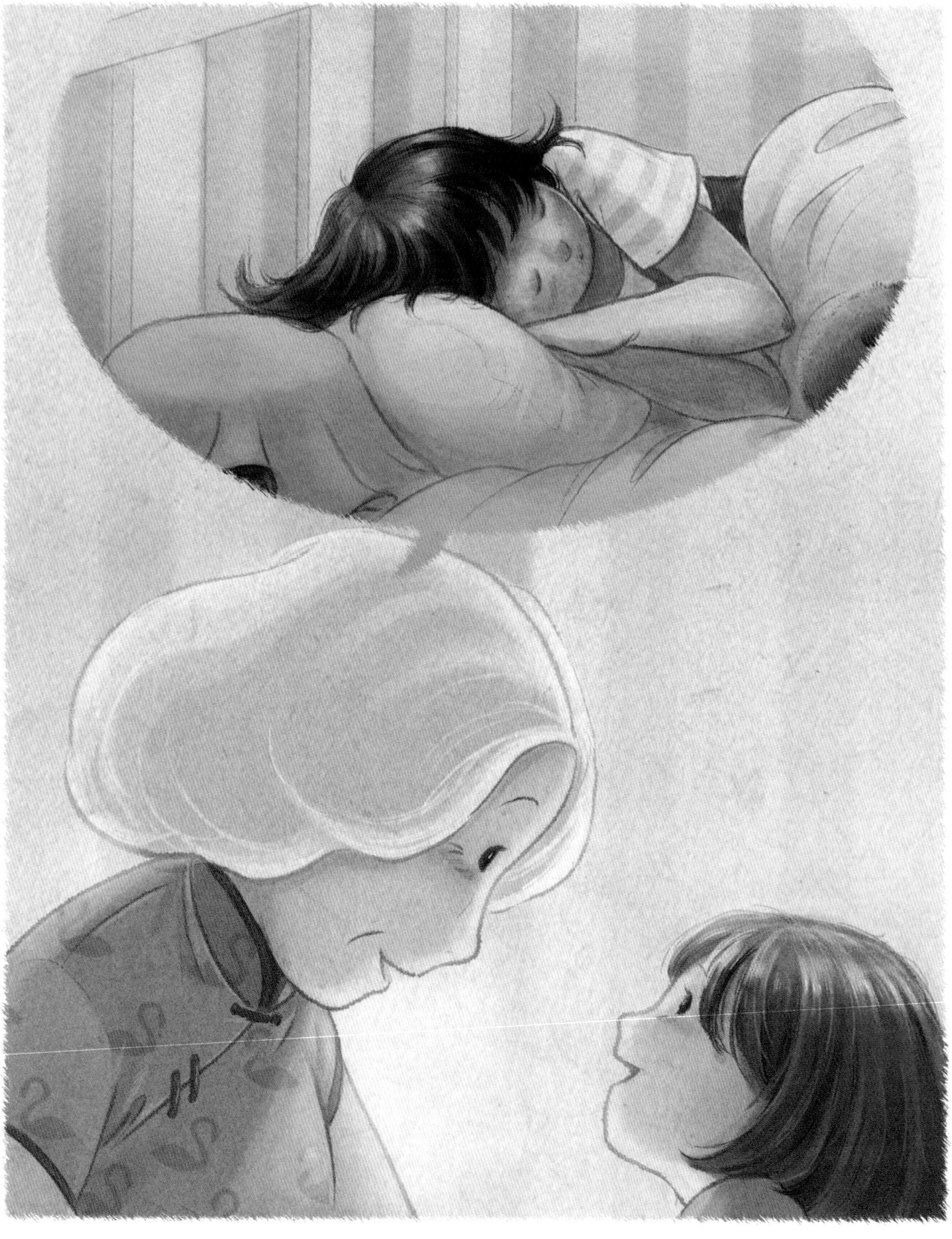

"Sleep well," Lao Lao said. "Tomorrow I'll tell you more."

"Lao Lao, did a turtle come out of the girl's egg too?"

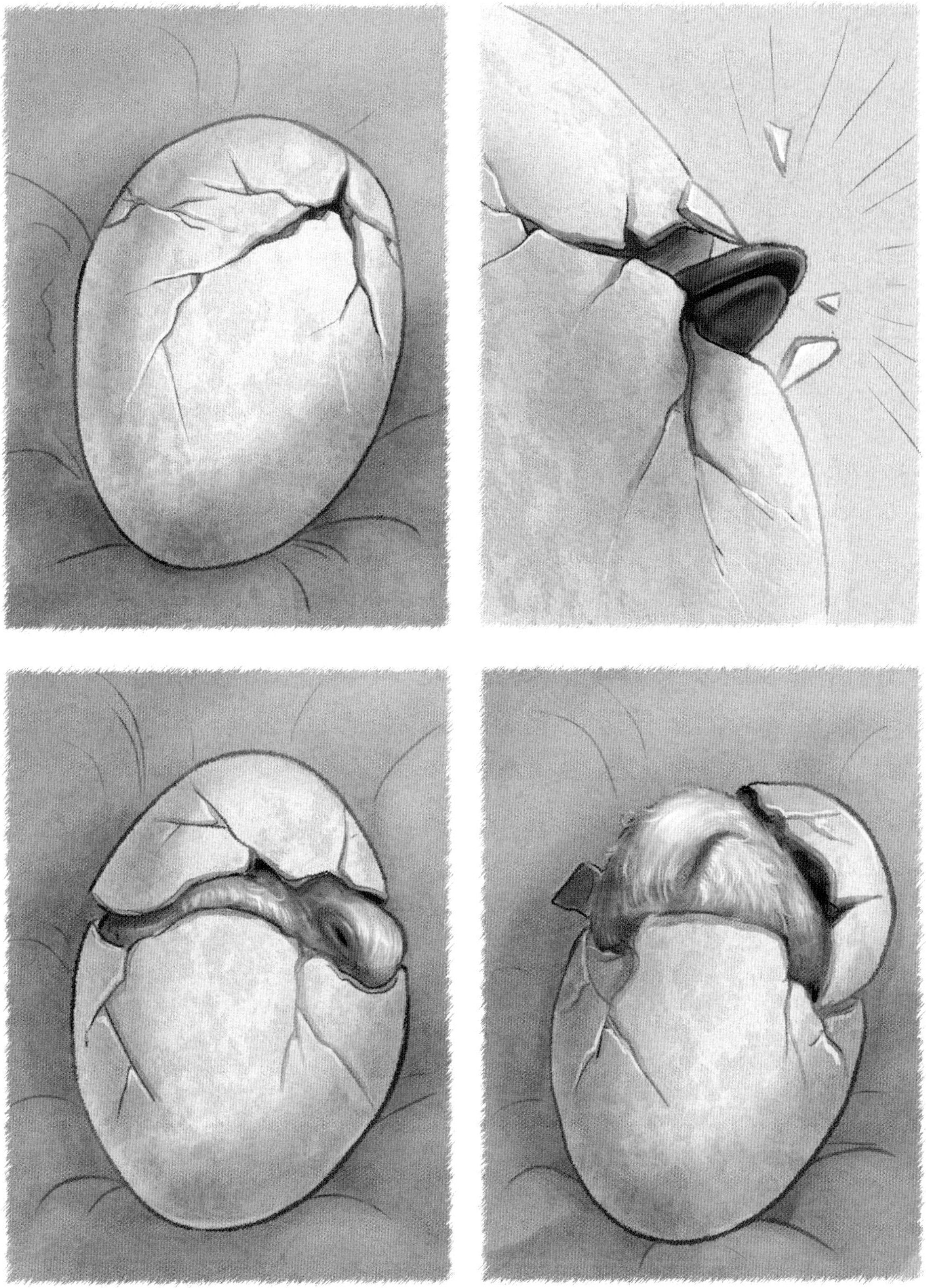

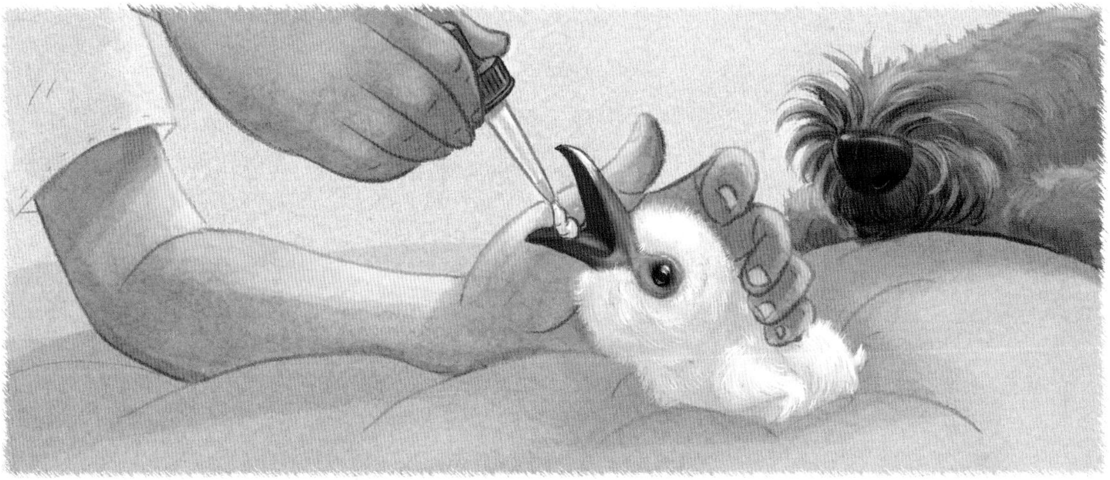

"They watched the sunset," said Lao Lao,
"but now we must head home."

"Lao Lao, can you tell me more about the girl and her flamingo?"

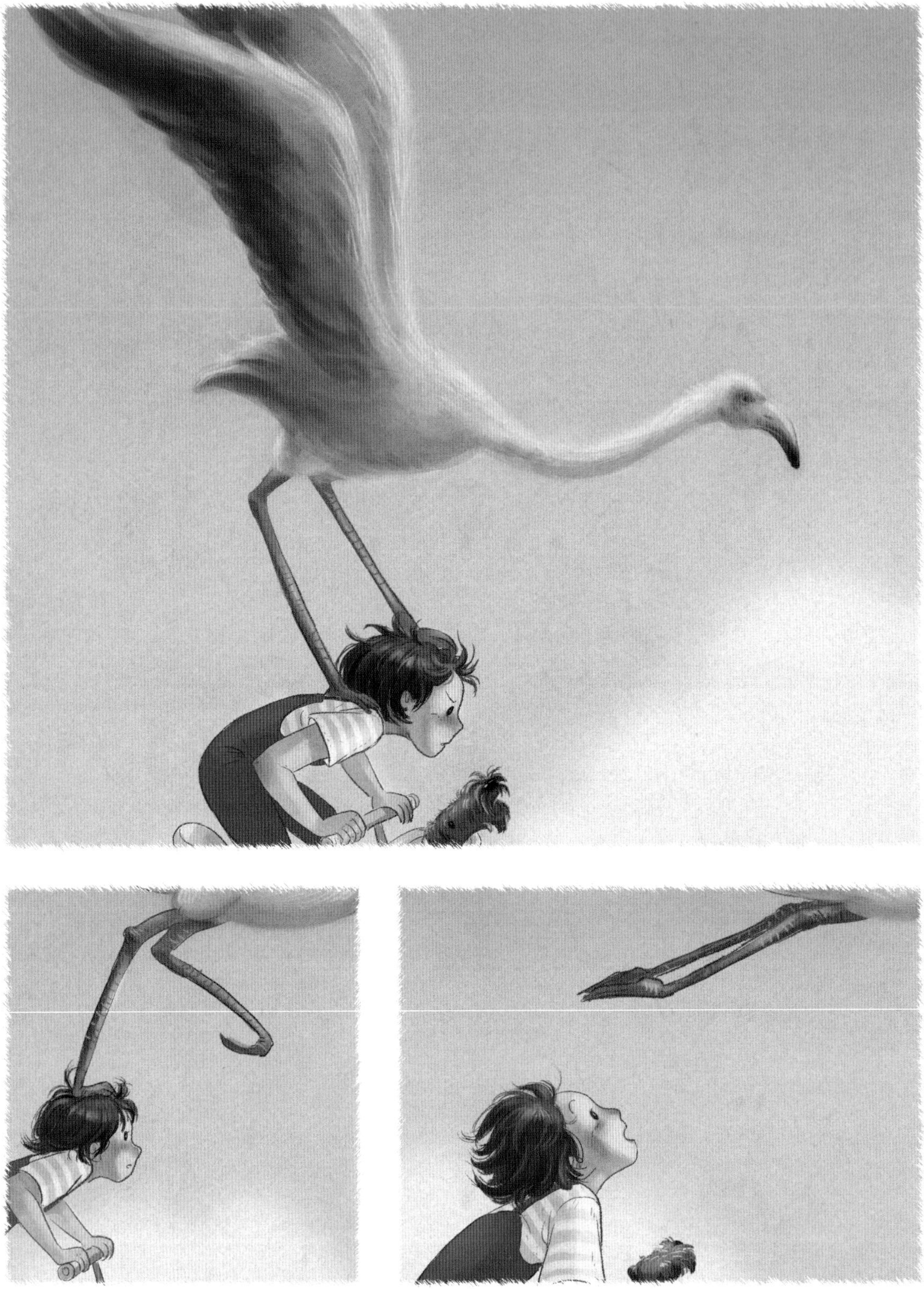

"And the girl rode home, her arms stretched wide," Lao Lao finished.

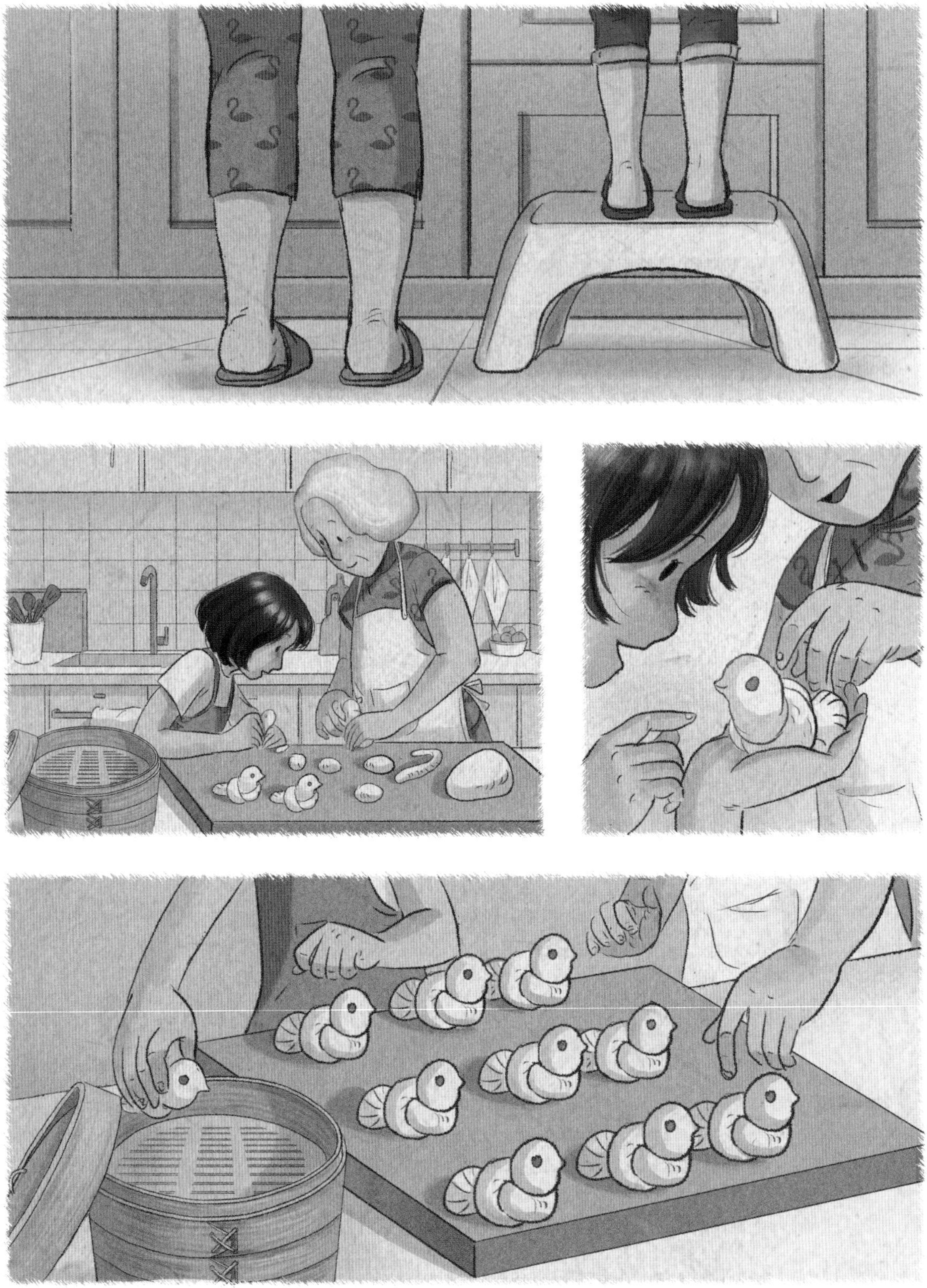

"Please tell me more, Lao Lao. Did the flamingo come back?"

"And the girl waited and hoped that someday
her friend would return."

part two

My Turn to Fly Home

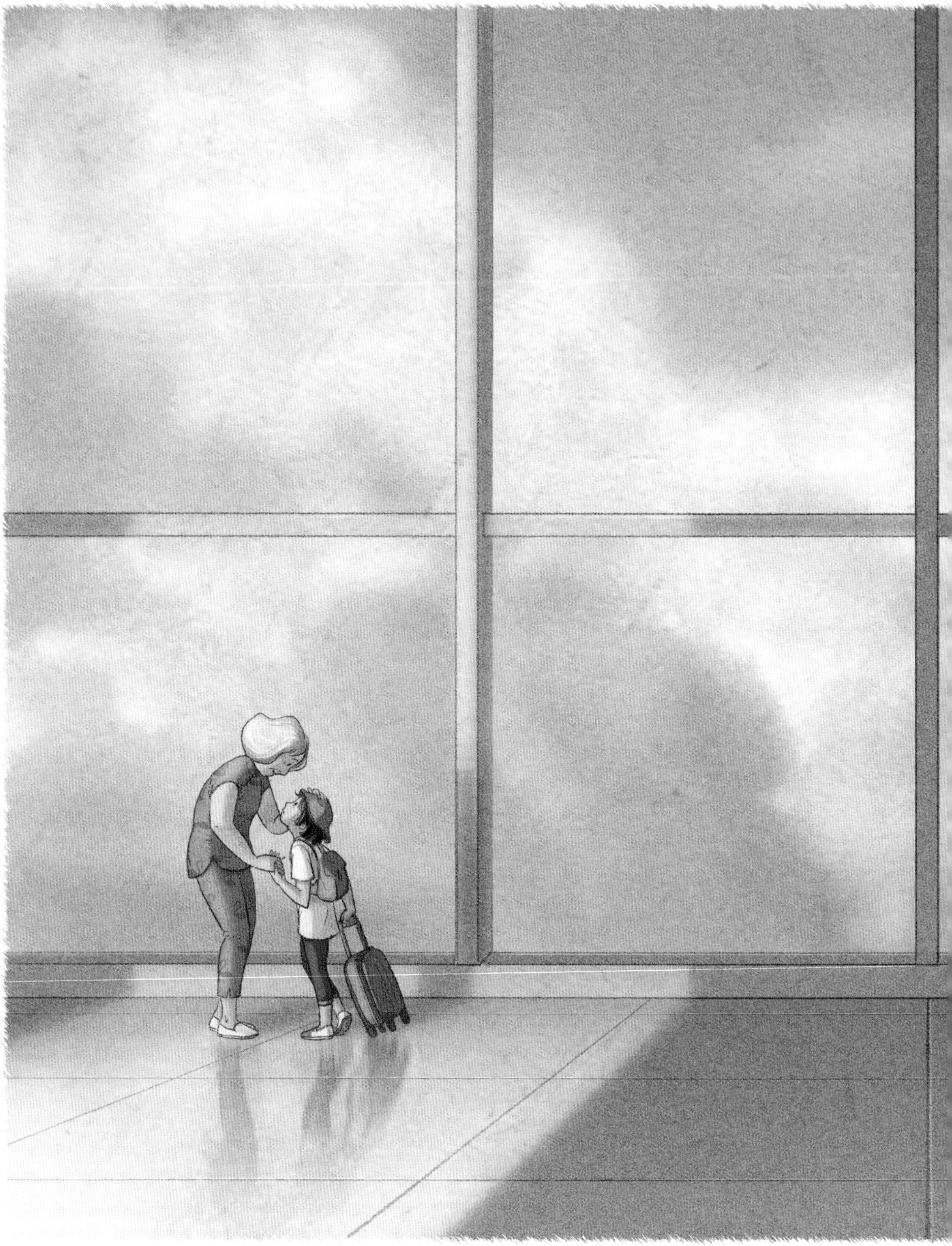

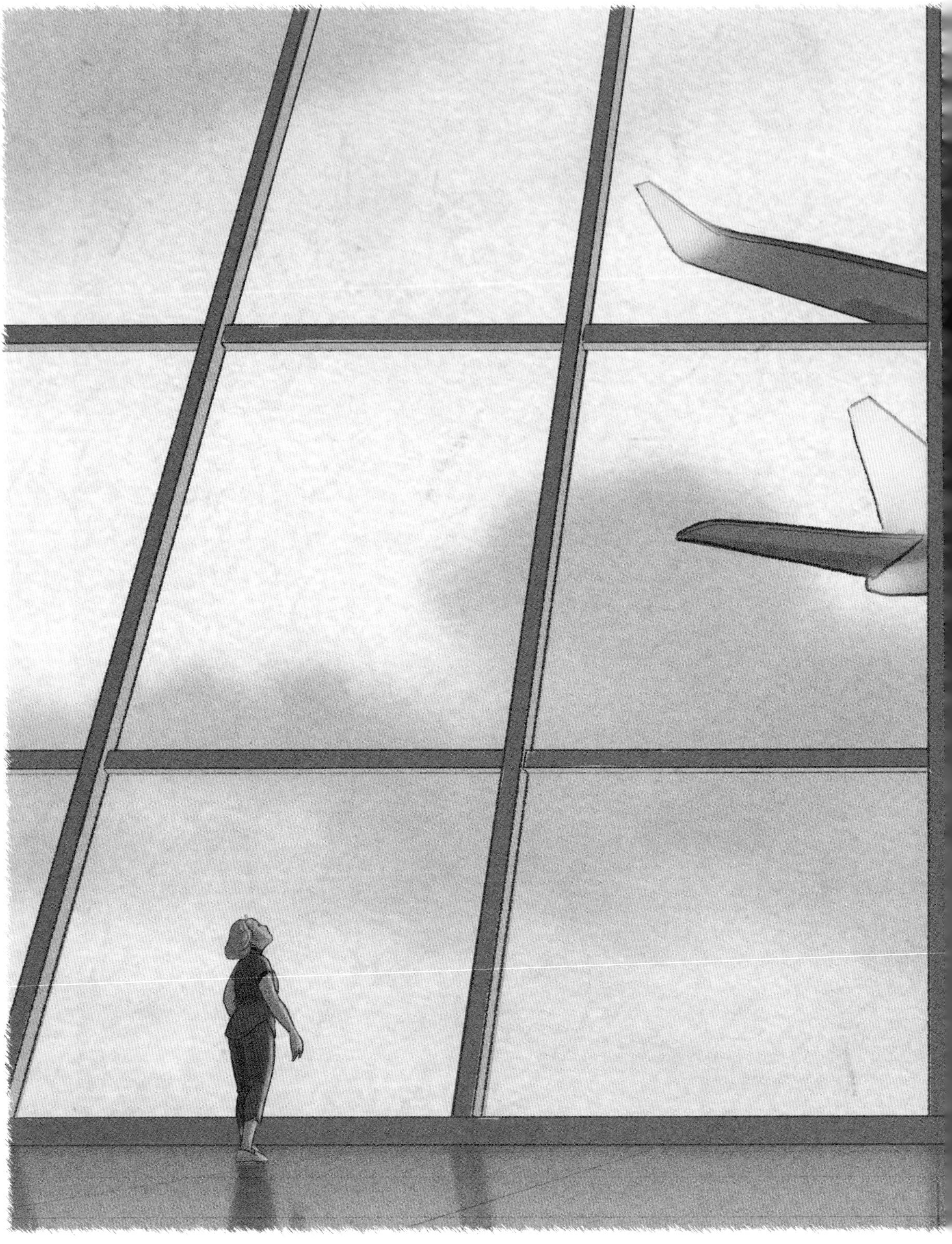

Arrivals

T

5 ST
ONE WAY

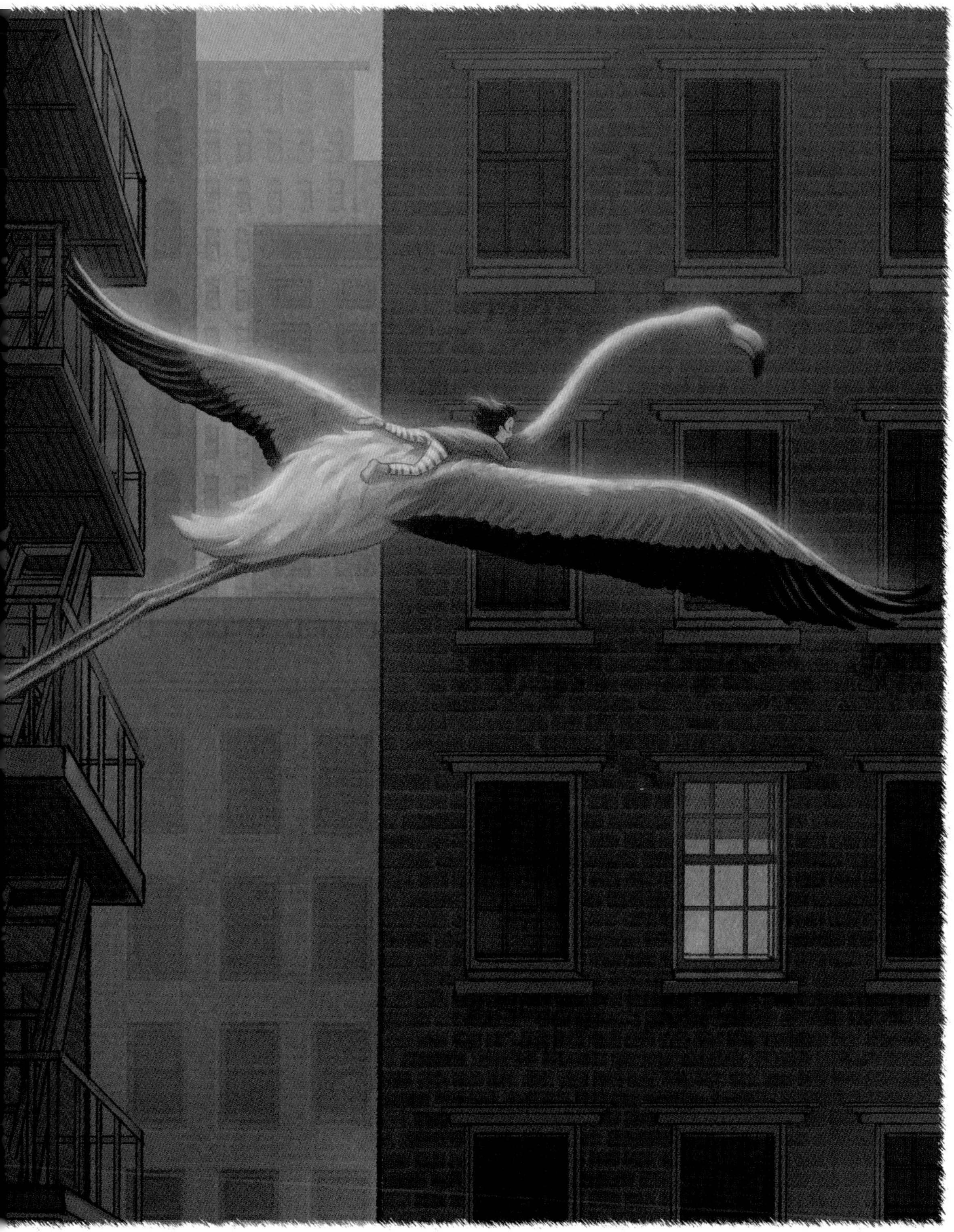

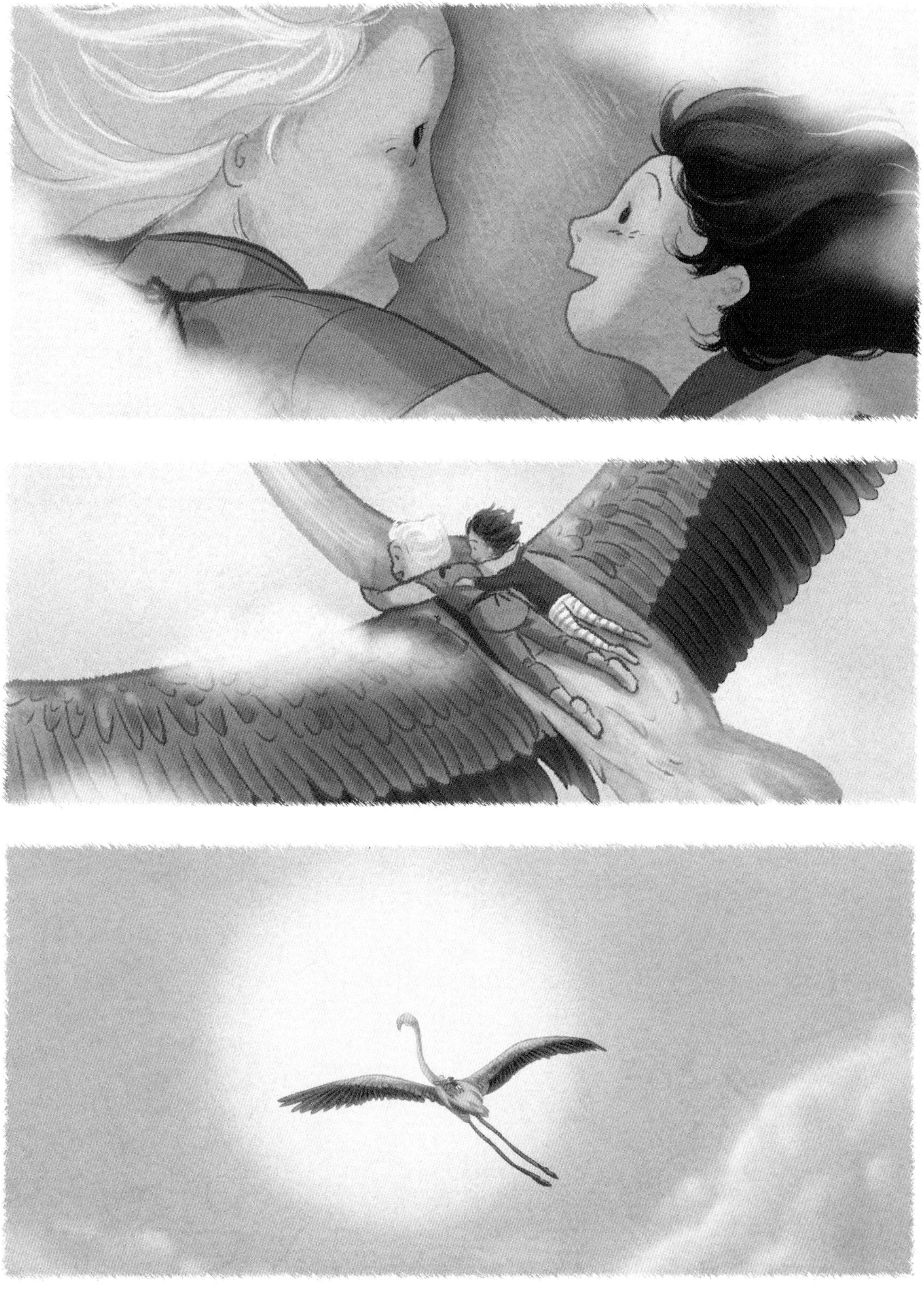

FOR
Lao Lao

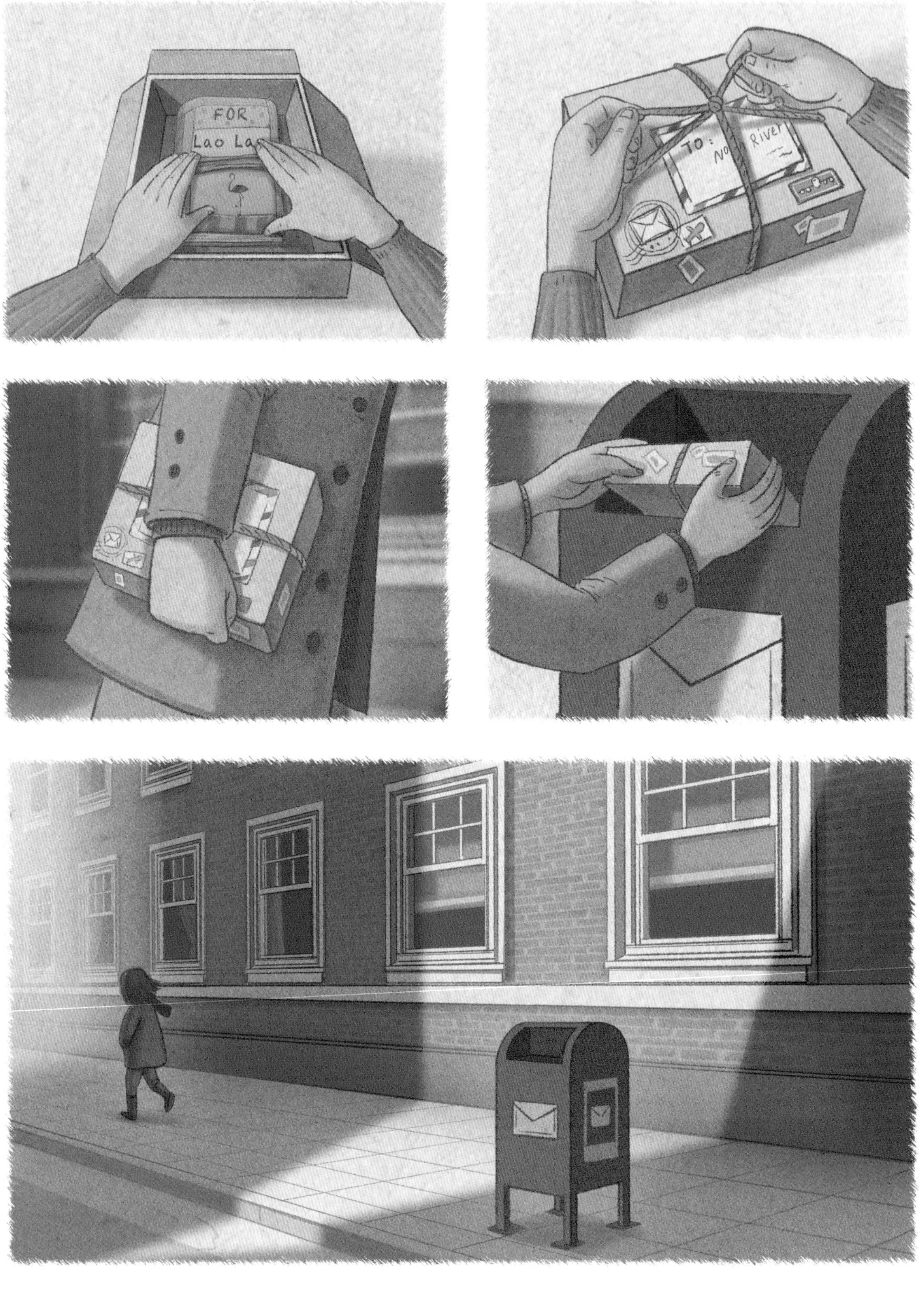
FOR
Lao La
TO:
River

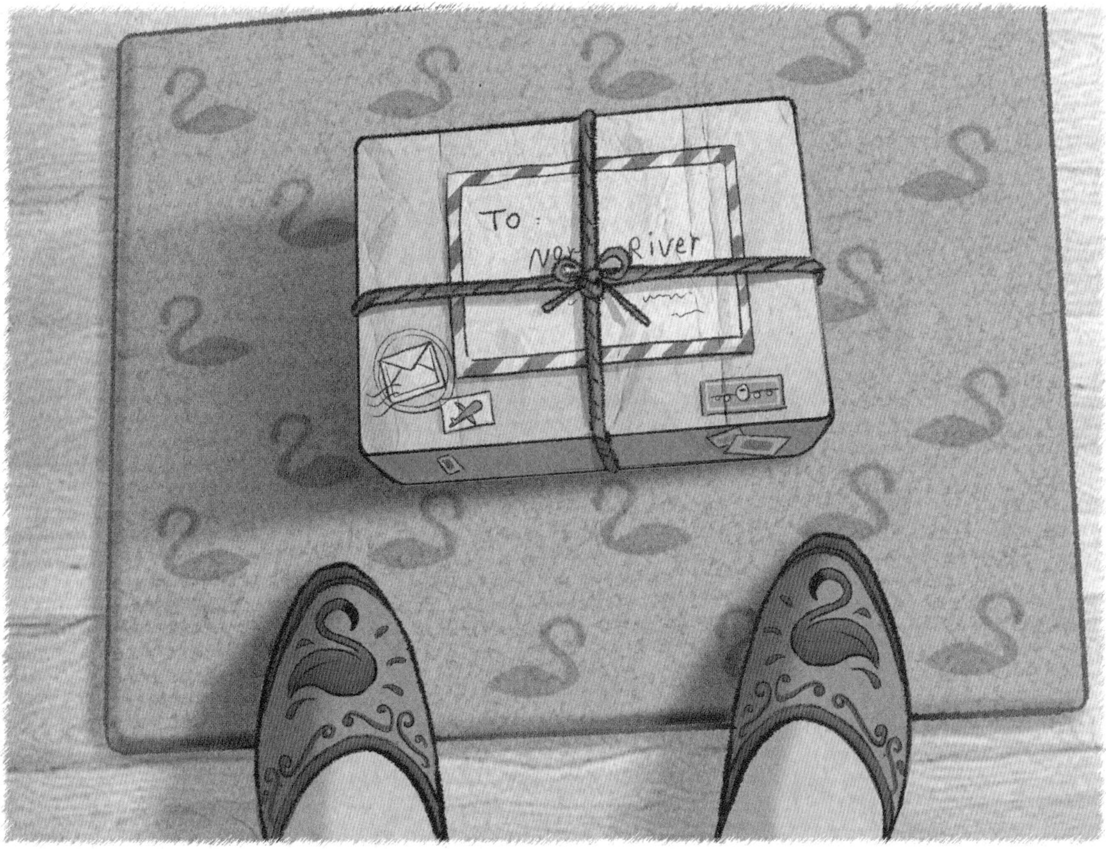
To :
River

FOR
Lao Lao

FOR
Lao Lo
FOR
Lao Lo

FOR
Lao

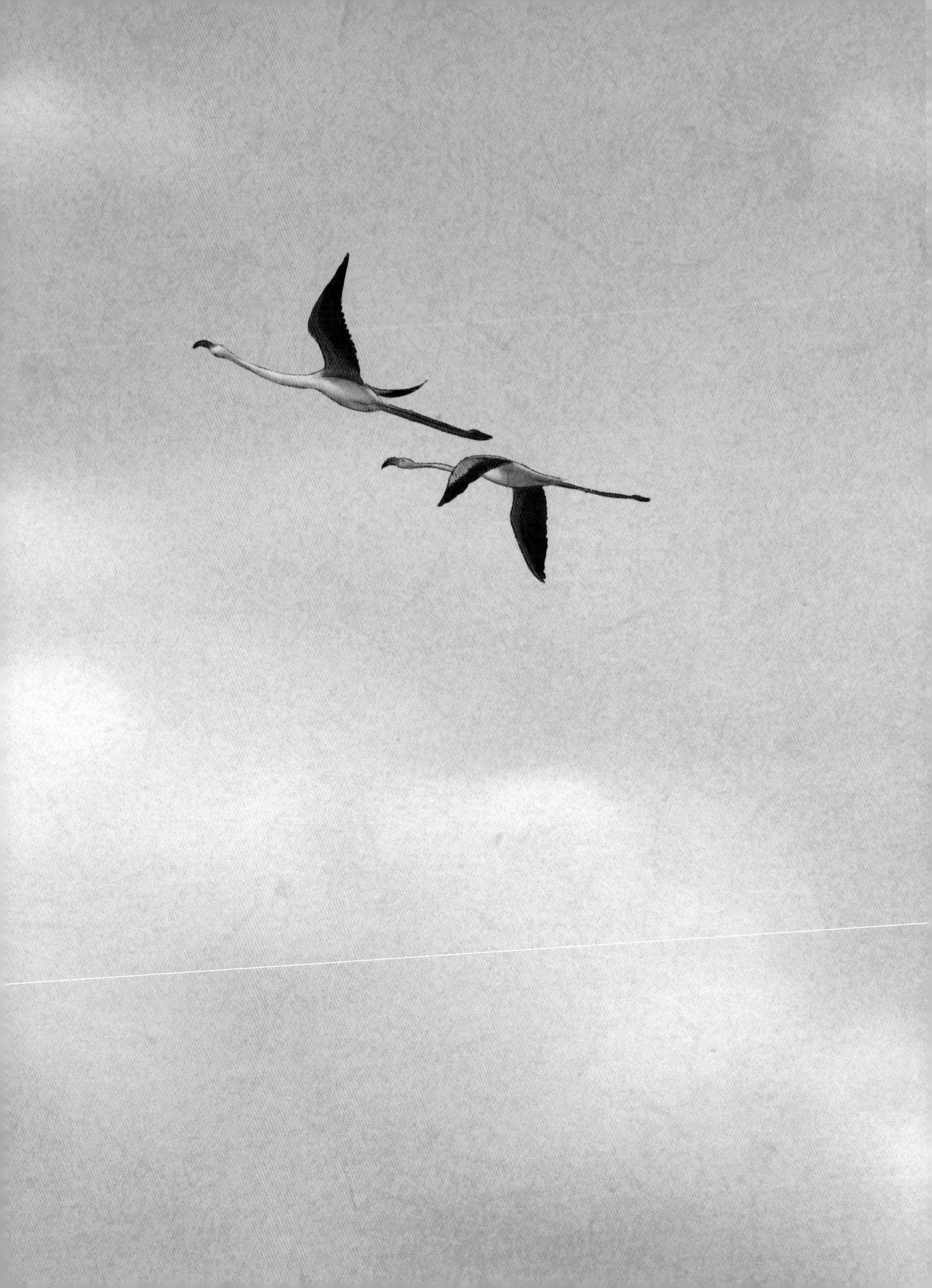